KUNTALINI

NEW LOVERS is a series devoted to
publishing new works of erotica
that explore the complexities
bedevilling contemporary
life, culture, and
art today.

OTHER TITLES IN THE SERIES
How to Train Your Virgin
We Love Lucy
God, I Don't Even Know Your Name
My Wet Hot Drone Summer
I Would Do Anything For Love
Burning Blue

KUNTALINI

×

TAMARA FAITH BERGER

**BADLANDS UNLIMITED
NEW LOVERS
Nº 7**

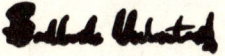

Kuntalini
by Tamara Faith Berger

New Lovers No. 7

Published by:
Badlands Unlimited LLC
operator@badlandsunlimited.com
www.badlandsunlimited.com

Series editors: Paul Chan, Ian Cheng, Micaela Durand, Matthew So
Copy editor: Charlotte Carter
Editorial assistant: Parker Bruce
Paper book designer: Carly Loman
Ebook designer: Micaela Durand
Front cover design by Kobi Benzari
Endpaper art by Paul Chan
Special thanks to Luke Brown, Elisa Leshowitz, Marlo Poras
The author wishes to thank Rosa Pagano, Lise Soskolne, Clement Virgo

Paper book distributed in the Americas by:
ARTBOOK | D.A.P. USA
155 6th Avenue, 2nd Floor
New York, NY 10013
Tel. +1 800 338 BOOK
www.artbook.com

Paper book distributed in Europe by:
Buchhandlung Walther König
Ehrenstrasse 4ß
50672 Köln
www.buchhandlung-walther-koenig.de

All rights reserved. No part of this publication may be reproduced, stored in retrieval systems, or transmitted in any form by any means, electronic, mechanical, photocopying, recording, psychic, interplanetary, or otherwise, without prior permission from the copyright holder.

Copyright © 2016 Badlands Unlimited

Printed in the United States of America

ISBN: 78-1-936440-95-5
E-Book ISBN: 978-1-936440-96-2

www.badlandsunlimited.com

CONTENTS

Chapter 1: Awake	1
Chapter 2: Obstacle	27
Chapter 3: Locomotion	47
Chapter 4: Youth	79
Chapter 5: Purge	113
Chapter 6: Gorge	125
About the Author	159

Chapter 1
Awake

This body is inert and flawed by its bad odors, odors arising from the flesh.

—*Hymn to the Kundalini*

It happened in yoga halfway through the class. My leggings stuck to me, leggings too thick to show dimples, and my bum itched from three nights of Indian food. I'd been shitting too much, shitting loose. Women slumped sweaty six inches apart in the pink-walled room of wood chip incense. We were finally on our asses after all the standing up. Sometimes yoga just doesn't feel good.

"*Pachimottanasana*, ladies. Open those cheeks!"

Jay-Jay, our teacher, barked into his headset over monotonous trance music beats. He wanted us to grab our own bum cheeks and move them apart before we went into our forward bends. Jay-Jay, a former gymnast, could fly up into handstand and do a jump-back from crossed-legs. Women loved him in yoga because he made them sweat hard; they loved his cut limbs and geometric tattoos. I worked on my forward bend really slowly so that my ass didn't chafe against my yoga pants.

"Oh ladies, *c'mon!*" Jay-Jay scolded.

He was watching me from across the room. "Don't just sit there and rock from side to side!"

I smelled plastic mat fungus. The music suddenly stopped. In the middle of the room, Jay-Jay demonstrated: he planted his legs hip-width apart and basically just snapped in half.

"What I want you to do is split your buns, girls. Like *this*."

Hanging over his legs, Jay-Jay's sitting bones protruded. His sandy blond hair swept down to his toes. Jay-Jay reached up and around to snatch his own butt. That ass had no fat. You could see every muscle and ligament of him. With his ass cheeks apart and spine dangling, Jay-Jay made a little *yum* sound. His pose was impressive. The music returned.

Jay-Jay bolted up smiling and adjusted his shorts. His plucked chest was slick with bubbles of sweat. I spotted his cock sucked in spandex, crescent hung. He made every person in that class rip themselves open from scratch.

I was irritated. Itchy. I didn't want to do it again.

Jay-Jay surveyed the room. He yelled at me: "*Yoo-hoo*, over there, don't just rock from side to side!"

Why me? I was not rocking. I was trying to avoid this chafing pain.

Jay-Jay marched through the bodies and stood by my mat.

"*Dandasana*, people," he barked. "Sit it back up. Spines tall and chins tucked. *Yoo-hoo*, you need help."

Jay-Jay's veined calves loomed in my

peripheral vision. Did he really just call me *Yoo-hoo*?

I wanted to leave this fucking greenhouse. I wanted a beer. Yoga didn't always work. Hamish told me to just stop feeling guilty about that.

Jay-Jay straddled my mat behind me. Then he squatted. He actually sucked his teeth. He was *mad*? So everyone but me knew how to split themselves in half?

"Yes, ladies!" Jay-Jay screamed. I couldn't see what was going on. "This is what I'm talking about! Forward bend, yes, people! All the way down."

Jay-Jay touched my low back to signal that he was going to give me an adjustment. I'd had adjustments from him before but this was different.

Jay-Jay hissed, "Come on, girl. Back

up. I just have to do it for you."

He made that irritated sucking sound again. I'd spread my fucking cheeks but I was in *pain*. I had a *blister* in my asshole. All week I'd shit loose. I really just wanted to get up and leave. Suck a beer top. Chomp chips. But I was trapped in this pseudo-exercise class where people were trying to burn off toxins or whatever. Jay-Jay roughly shovelled his palms underneath me. I felt a sharp tear between my ass cheeks. I immediately seized.

"Wait," I said. "That hurts."

But Jay-Jay didn't stop what he was doing. He tightened his grip on each half of my sweaty yoga pant ass.

"When I say out to each side, I mean *out to each side*."

The tips of his pinky fingers actually pushed into my ass crack. He kept spreading me until I thought I would bleed. My asshole felt striated, taut. A poker burn. I really didn't have a second. Jay-Jay picked me up like that—right off my mat —and tipped me forward. I felt weightless. I was holding my breath.

"Don't," I said into myself.

That ripping hot poker sensation shot right up inside me.

"*Stop*," I said, louder.

But he was not listening to me. Trance beats filled the room, like we were all in a club. I smelled everyone's brine. And Jay-Jay barked out more directions while he stayed with me, lifting and prodding my raw asshole *on purpose*. I could not believe it. This wasn't a regular adjustment.

"Put me down," I hissed. "*Please*."

Still gripping my ass, Jay-Jay finally set me down on my mat.

"And that is how you do it, ladies! *Pachimottanasana* bliss!"

With my head on my shins I huffed in my own breaths. I was mortified. Was he using me as an example? My asshole felt completely exposed; it was beating like an organ through my stuck leggings. In this butchered position, helpless, I thought Jay-Jay was done. I thought I could finally, somehow, just get up and leave, but then I felt this hot, unnatural nudge between my ass cheeks.

"Pose looks amazing," Jay-Jay whispered.

He was still over me, behind me, touching my ass. I was hog-tied. Jay-Jay's pinkies kept nudging. *Yoo-hoo.* My sweat smelled spicy. I could not breathe right.

KUNTALINI

It felt like something was peeping out of my anus, something coming to meet his knuckles, something from my ass had started to *protrude*. . . Something was fucking coming out of me back there! God, I felt like I had to shit! My sitting bones split. I felt sick. Something wiggled, there was this wiggling *thing*, a kind of nub tail, emerging from my asshole that burned and felt *wrong*. I'd shit too much. . . Jay-Jay's knuckles pushed in and *it* was pushing back out. His pressure was making that thing grow. My mouth opened. I panted. I licked my slick leggings. I needed to get out of this tight forward bend but Jay-Jay had clamped his knees at my hips.

"Yeah, you're heating up now, aren't you?"

My pussy pressed into my mat. That live wiggling nub in my ass was on fire. I felt weirdly turned on and desperate. Hamish, my boyfriend of over two years, barely liked to fuck anymore. It had been *three months* since we fucked. Now my clit was smashed flat in a yoga class. Now this ass nub, this hot split, had been forced on me. Was it clear to my teacher that I was pulsing everywhere? Jay-Jay was *gay*. What the fuck was he doing to me?

"I need to get up," I panted into my legs.

Jay-Jay slithered *on top of me*. What the fuck, I'd just told him I needed to get up! The guy's naked chest pinned down my back. The wiggling in my asshole was way too much sensation. I wanted it to stop. I felt Jay-Jay's nipples, sharp points searing into my back. And then his crescent cock replaced his knuckles, his tough crescent cock lodged there at my crack. The wiggling in my ass became a little pig's tail. My little pig's tail was touching his hose.

"Keep it coming, girl, keep it coming out. . ."

"No," I whined. I wanted to scream.

The music droned. I thought everyone in the studio could hear me.

"Yoo-hoo has an open ass," Jay-Jay whispered right into my ear. His breath smelled like tea tree. "Come on, girl, come on. Keep opening up."

Why was he doing this? Why was he holding me down? He was hurting me. I could not open anymore! My ass and my cunt felt totally fused. They were trading sparks. I was stuck. I was buzzing. Then Jay-Jay humped me once—and it *wagged*. Yeah, the tail-thing moved. That actually felt good. I mean, suddenly some of the discomfort was gone. My nub started pulsing, throbbing; it felt like this backwards clit-like protrusion. Jay-Jay humped it again. His cock stuck. I started to shake. I knew I was going to come. It felt really good. I was really going to come.

"Stop it," Jay-Jay ordered. "Come on. Let it rise."

I sweat into him and into my pants. Face-smashed, I frothed out bubbles of sweat. *Rise?* The feelings coming out of my ass were almost unbearable. I was shaking all over. I wanted his cock inside my ass. He kept humping his pubic bone into me, these hard, quick thrusts with the pipe of his cock. I could feel my clit pulse, my pig's clit, my ass split in half. It all made me crazy, but I could not rise. What did he mean, *rise*? Everything in me felt trapped, all his humping heat secret. I could not scream in yoga. I just really wanted to come!

Hamish said that my body had changed since he'd known me. He said that I had a bubble butt now. He used to like to slap it when we had sex; our favorite position was doggy-style. I didn't know what happened with us, why we weren't having sex. I'd never had a cock all the way in my asshole and it occurred to me right then that Hamish wanted to fuck my blooming ass. If it felt like this, yes, Hamish had to fuck my ass!

Jay-Jay heaved more weight onto me. I thought for a second I was going to pass out. His cock was a metal pipe stuck between my ass cheeks, my *center*, where I could usually squeeze, but I was spread so wide there, so split there, that I couldn't do a thing. I just had to take it.

"Yoo-hoo," Jay-Jay whispered. "Go further. Take your toes."

In the buzzing damp dark of the yoga studio I realized my teacher was really calling me *Yoo-hoo*. My name was Yoo-hoo. I couldn't feel my fucking toes. For a second it was as if my whole body had disappeared. All I was, was ass. All I had was tail. His cock and my tail. We were joined in a room of dripping female pits. I wanted to strip off my leggings. Expose myself. Shake it. Yoga overheats. I could take a cock in my ass. Hamish's cock, stubby and hot. *Fuck my ass*, I'd tell him. *Baby, split my tight ass.* I wanted everyone to fuck me. I was going further, *rising*. I felt my hands meet my toes. I hooked my toes with my thumb and first finger. I was grasping, I was buzzing, I was really alive! I wanted Jay-Jay to hump my crack. Pull my tail. Put it in. *God, put it in!* It felt so fucking good. I shook my head into my legs.

"The fire's building, Yoo-hoo. Let the fire build."

I heard Jay-Jay laugh. Then I felt him sort of slide down my back and rearrange himself.

No, no. Don't leave. Don't leave me like this!

The music faded. I had cotton balls in my ears. I was dizzy and plugged up. I didn't even know if Jay-Jay was still on top of me or not. Something was happening. I heard three chimes and women chanting *Om Shanti Om*. My eyes were squeezed shut. I could not move. I felt people rolling up their sticky mats around me.

"Is she okay?" I heard someone say.

I was trembling. They could all see my ass.

"She'll be fine," Jay-Jay said.

Hamish would be waiting downstairs for me. We were supposed to go to brunch.

"*Namaste*, ladies."

The room emptied. I kept shaking.

"I need to go," I mewled inside this

ass-raw forward bend.

That really made him laugh. I tried to take a deep breath. I needed to make my voice louder. Hair covered my eyes. There was a prickly, beating bud in my ass. I was totally paralyzed.

"Jay-Jay, I can't get up!" I shrieked.

Suddenly I was lifted up off my mat. Jay-Jay was right there and he yanked down my leggings. Oh my god, all my limbs were asleep. I heard myself hyperventilating. I wanted to shit. Red bud, pig's tail. I felt it all over again. Tail wagging. Tail on fire. It was *big*. It wasn't a corkscrew anymore! My pants were tied at my knees, halfway pulled down. Jay-Jay could see it. I knew he could see it.

A door closed. The lights dimmed.

"My *boyfriend*," I whimpered.

I felt this snake-like inner twisting from my ass to my cunt.

"Please," I begged. "Do something!"

I was mortified at the sound of myself. I was terrified that I had a hemorrhoidal spread. He was looking at my monkey ass, examining me from behind. I felt all alone, my breath short.

"Just breathe, Yoo-hoo, *breathe*."

I breathed. I was trying! But my ass tail's being looked at had started a spark. That spark shot up my clit and invaded my gut. I freaked. *This* was rising! My lips opened. I drooled. I let the heat circle and rise from my ass. First from my ass to my clit, then my clit to my navel, my navel to my ribs, yeah, a flame on each rib. My ass was on fire! My entire body shaking. Hog-tied. Dark ass. God, where was Jay-Jay? Where was Hamish? I was totally ready to explode!

"That's it," Jay-Jay crooned from somewhere above me. "*This* is what I'm talking about."

There was something inside me, something electric and loose with no apparent relationship to me. For the first time in my life I felt like I had an inner being.

Fuck me. Fuck me. My breaths were so shallow. *Fuck me. Fuck it.* My clit beat in time. I was numb, nearly numb, from the white-hot heat at my ass. Then I felt Jay-Jay. I didn't know where he was.

"I'm touching the vital chord," Jay-Jay said.

This was it. He lay behind me on the mat, his long blond hair streaming out.

His mouth was open at my split, swollen ass. Jay-Jay stuck out his tongue. His tongue flicked my tail.

"Noooo," I moaned. "Yessss!"

I was way too far gone.

Jay-Jay flicked me once. Then he licked all around my tail. He had this fishy tongue, like a fish flopping around. I huffed into my legs. *Excruciation.* Tongue knew what it was doing. It found my tail, licked it. My bung hole, Jay-Jay stuffed his tongue inside it. It wasn't easy. Tongue was cold. I clutched inside as hard as I could with my way-too-split-open ass.

"Good, good. Gape, *c'mon*, open up."

Jay-Jay got into this rhythm, this insane flick and push in, then this random rimming, then pulling out for more spit. My asshole twitched. Then it twisted. I loved it so much. I wanted to cry. Gaping meant *open*. How could I stay open back there and release my own clutch? No one had ever done anything like this to me—this concentration, the long build, all the heat, all the wetness. It was amazing, his tongue in and out, spit-rimming my asshole, tail wagging, monkey hairs, I was just about to come, I couldn't hold myself back anymore, this time, right here, I was really going to come. My innards burned with radiator heat. I let myself gape. I was never going to shit. God, Hamish was waiting. Gape. Let it *open*. This gape in my ass felt *better* than my pussy. Tongue pushed inside it. I hadn't stopped shaking. His tongue played with my tail. Gape. This was *it*, I loved *it*! My asshole treated and tongued. This was *it*, this was *me*! His tongue jammed inside me now, taut, fully stuck. The ultimate itch in my tail exploded. I felt wetness like pee. One sharp shot torpedoed up to my head.

"Motherfucker," Jay-Jay panted.

I laughed hysterically. Tears came out. No head. Breath everywhere. That was a backward orgasm! A gunshot. Jay-Jay kept licking but he was miles away. Heat trickled out of my asshole for him.

"Nectar," Jay slurped. "Radiance."

I could not recover as he nosed me. I was still folded in half. Maybe I'd never stop vibrating like this, trickling like this, gaping like this. Nectar. One ass. My little hog tail. Maybe this was me now: *Yoo-hoo*.

I heard Jay-Jay moaning. I finally moved my head to the left. My head was the first thing that moved in the bend after the red hot monkey heat shot through my skull. Jay-Jay had rolled a few feet away. He was rubbing his cock, jerking on his side, frigging up and down faster than I'd ever seen a guy do. His tongue was erect. His whole body shook. All his slick muscles glistened. *Autoerotic*. Sticky blond hair. Jay-Jay's eyes rolled. I was still not upright. And his frequency hit me like lightning; I received one more shot. Jay-Jay shook and he stiffened. I touched my wet leggings that were sagged at my knees. I got a second ass spasm: more gush and more heat. *Om* Yogi Jay-Jay! We moaned at the same time. His cock expelled three great stringings of cum. One shot hit my face, the corner of my lips. The rest pooled on my yoga mat's corner. His cum smelled like firecracker fray. I started laughing.

"Dana, is that you? Are you in there?"

Hamish rapped at the studio door. I was licking my lips. Jay-Jay's jism tasted burnt sugar sweet. I had to get up, peel my torso off my legs. I tried to yank up my slick leggings still sitting down, licking. I couldn't do it. Sticky jism. My leggings were stuck. My pussy was huge. It dripped onto my thighs. I had droplets like Jay-Jay's, translucent sweat. He rolled around on the floor, slit-eyed, smiling at me.

"Motherfucker," he said again. "Yoo-hoo, you're *it*."

My hand slipped in his puddle of cum as I pushed myself finally to standing and tried to pull up my yoga pants.

"Dana, are you there?"

My legs trembled. "Yeah, I'm here. One second, just a sec."

I smeared my lips with Jay-Jay's fresh jizz. I wanted to bow down and lick the rest off my mat. Jay-Jay laughed at me stumbling around like a newborn calf. I whimpered. I needed the wall for support. I could not go on feeling like this. Clit stiff and an ass tail burning up my inner being.

"*Yoo-hoo*," Jay-Jay whispered from the floor. I turned. "Yoo-hoo, you're leaking radiance."

Yeah, I felt that. Light was dripping through my pants. For a second, I thought I could feel *everything*. Hamish would feel this new energy in me. He'd fuck me tonight. Jay-Jay rolled away. I collected my cummed-on yoga mat and supported myself along the wall all the way to the door, to my boyfriend who was waiting for me.

Chapter 2
Obstacle

A condition of horror, on account of the inexplicable change, began to settle on me.

—*Gopi Krishna*

Hamish hugged me at the studio door, his belly pressed against my ribs. I felt this membrane of sex, a new musky goo. Hamish grabbed my wet ass and squeezed it hard. This was the most affectionate he'd been with me in months.

My sphincter instinctively went into fresh spasms. My leggings were sopping. I felt overwhelmed. Hamish was as big as Sasquatch, nuclear hair all over his chest. His beard smelled like pot. My boyfriend was an anomaly in a yoga studio. He played bass in *Goatse*, a death metal band.

"Dana, why are your pants so fucking wet?"

I was breathing too fast and I felt an urge to run away and shit.

"Come on. We're *late*."

I wriggled out of his hammy grip. I didn't know how I going to go to brunch with his buddies fielding orgasms in my ass.

"I have to shower first," I said.

In the shower I could stuff my fingers inside me. I could feel my tail for the first time.

"For fuck's sake, Dana. We don't have time for you to shower."

Leaning against the Yoga Toes display, I tried to catch my breath. Jay-Jay was in the studio, right behind that door.

"What is up with you, Dana? Your face looks all swollen."

"Hamish," I whispered, tail buzzing, "do you think we're ever going to have sex again?"

Hamish flinched. "Why did you have to just ruin our Sunday? *Fuck*."

Hamish walked to the top of the stairs. My throat felt unnaturally tight.

"Because you're my *boyfriend*, Hamish." I felt like I was going to cry.

Hamish always got mad when I asked him anything directly. He even stormed out sometimes when I was upset. I needed to be able to tell my boyfriend what I wanted! I felt so needy and weak with him, and I'd just felt so amazing. *You have to ask him to go down on you,* my friends said to me. *He's not just going to do it on his own.* Hamish didn't ever want to lick my pussy, or maybe he didn't know how to lick my pussy, but it occurred to me, on the verge of tears, that I actually needed more than pussy-licking now. I needed pussy-sucking. Pussy-swallowing. Full-on rimming. Anal sex. I wanted jism to swim up my sphincter, I wanted great shots of cum to plaster my ass. I wanted to gape and take jism. I wanted jism for tears.

"For fuck's sake, Dana. What are you crying about?"

I covered my eyes. I felt like his dumb

girlfriend bitch.

Then Jay-Jay emerged from the studio. He strutted out like a peacock, tits hard. He eyed Hamish and me. I wanted to fall down on my knees. I wanted to go back to how we just were — enraptured, in bliss, all my new asshole sensations. . .

As if on cue, I started to sob.

"Jesus Christ, Dana. Let's get the fuck out of here. *Now*."

A vein in Jay-Jay's forehead beat prominently. Hamish stormed up to me and grabbed the strap of my yoga mat bag. He yanked me backwards towards the stairs. My ass started to shake.

"*Yoo-hoo*," my teacher whispered.

I turned around. I stared at Jay-Jay's bulging eyes, his exaggerated lashes. *Rescue me*, I thought. But Jay-Jay just stared at me and Hamish with no expression on his face, as if he hadn't just called me, as if he hadn't just licked out my asshole. Jay-Jay waltzed into his office and shut the door behind him. I was embarrassed about how much I'd just felt.

"Hamish," I said, "I don't feel so good."

All that ass play, that pleasure, was just totally gone.

"Dana, you *never* feel good."

I *never* feel good? I tried to steady myself. That wasn't true. *Fuck*. I followed Hamish down the studio stairs, my ass cheeks feeling like blubber. In the shoe room, I put on my burgundy sandals with the little kitten heels. Outside on the street, sun shocked my watery eyes. What in the world had just happened to me? I squinted at girls in their short skirts and wedge heels. Why did we all wear bad shoes for fun? Sweat dripped down my temples. My face was drenched. Girls always dressed to turn everyone on. God, I felt nauseous. My tits smashed together in my wet yoga tank like a package of beef.

Dizzy, wiping my eyes, I realized that Hamish was gone. I started to trot down the sidewalk to our brunch spot, feeling weights in my pants, spasms in my calves. Why was Hamish now rejecting me too? This was abusive. I was limping, loping. It was two o'clock in the afternoon. I pushed my way past the brunch line outside our haunt. By the time I got back to the patio, Hamish and his bandmates were sharing a spliff. Hamish ignored me but Arne and Idris watched me stumble in, leggings wet.

Idris was laughing, showing uneven teeth. He was the singer in *Goatse*. The guy had long black hair and prison-style tattoos on his neck. Idris was born in Mexico City, in a *slum*, Hamish said, always exaggerating that word. The guy had unpleasant eyes: catlike green slits with wiry eyebrows on an overhang. I could never look at Idris directly. Arne played keyboard. He was thick-jointed, dirty blond, harmless in comparison.

I slid into my seat. Hamish still hadn't looked at me. It was clear that he just wanted to get baked. The rockabilly waitress came over to our table. Idris offered her a drag of the oversized spliff. She took it. She knew them. The *Goatse* boys had been coming here for years.

"I'll have a pint of stout," I said to the waitress as she imprinted her too-red lipstick on the joint.

Idris tapped the waitress's ass. I felt chained to my chair. My ass flesh deadened. I hated Idris. He wrote misogynist lyrics. His music made me feel insane.

"Are you okay, Dana?" Arne said to me.

"She's all slutted up from yoga," Hamish said as he sucked on the lipsticked joint.

"Shut up, man," Arne said.

Why was Hamish making that connection—slut, yoga? Did he subconsciously realize after squeezing my sweaty yoga ass that I was all of a sudden sexually free?

Idris smiled at me, knuckles at his throat. "Give her a puff," he said.

I reached out for the joint Hamish was passively handing to me but Idris snatched it first. What a fuck head. Hamish snorted. He and Idris were aligned.

"Don't be mean to Dana," Arne said.

Idris focused on me, smoking. "Right. She needs this more than me."

I did not look back at Idris but he finally handed me the joint. I took two really deep pulls. Hamish always got hydroponic. And I felt better smoking. Immediately. I realized that I had this new privacy. A privacy inside. Then my beer came. I passed the joint over to Arne.

I downed half my pint in one gulp. "I'll take another," I said.

But our waitress was already gone. Fuck these metal heads. I had the urge to get stoned. My legs spread under the table. I felt the bite of sweet skunk flit around in my thighs. I rearranged my tits in my tank top just to feel my body again. Hamish eyed me and passed the spliff around the table once more.

"Don't give any more to Dana," Idris said.

Now I smirked. Fuck you, *goat*. My nipples were hard. Our waitress brought a bowl of corn chips to our table.

"Do you want to order food?" she asked me.

I wanted to pinch her jeaned-up vulva and finger her ass.

"Another beer," I said, looking at her clotted black lashes.

I wanted to forget that men existed and everything we did for them was *real*.

I chomped chips. I knew I needed to break up with my boyfriend. That was a hard thought to think. We were two years in and *living together*. Hamish looked like Action Bronson. He used to be a great kisser. I wanted a third hit of pot. A third beer. A third eye. Why wouldn't Hamish go down on me? Why did he have to make me feel like shit sexually? Was it him or was it me? Sometimes I really felt like it was me.

Fuck. The music raged. I sucked back the rest of my beer. I wanted to feel that slow build in my asshole again. The skill of Jay-Jay. A man's tongue on my tail. Pig's tail. Master wag. Yoga slut. All of that. I had to feel myself again. My tits, my cunt, *everything*. I slid off my chair and plopped down under the table. I felt pissed off and horny. I needed time to myself.

"Dana, what the fuck?" Hamish said, his mouth full of chips.

"Let her be, man," Arne countered. He waved at me under the table.

Gum littered the ground. My leggings stuck to it. I was happy under the table. Hamish had a gut full of beer. I rested my head on Arne's knee. Instinctively, Arne stroked my hair. Idris had both his hands on his thighs. Then he spread his legs slowly, showed me the weight of his sac. I was a little drunk, a little stoned. Idris wore hard boots. Arne's leg was very relaxing.

Hamish pounded his fist on the table. "Come on, Dana! Get off that nasty ground."

I wanted to stay where I was, nasty, with Arne's big hand on my head. Then his whole palm on my cheek. Soon, Arne's thick white first finger came into my mouth. I sucked it to the knuckle. I ignored Hamish above me. I ignored Idris's spread legs. I took Arne's thumb and put it in my mouth. It tasted like smoke. Arne rubbed his thumb and finger together in my mouth. Scandinavian-style. That felt really good.

"What the hell is she doing under there?"

"Slut penance," said Idris.

Goatse wisdom at its best.

I heard Idris unzip his black jeans to my left while Arne's thumb and finger moved around my inner cheeks. Arne was pushing out my cheeks and stretching my lips, smearing the outsides with my own spit. It felt hot. I felt hot there, hiding under the table. But I wasn't sure if things would happen again, like they did with Jay-Jay. I wasn't sure if I needed to be in a yoga pose for it to start. I mean, sex feelings in my ass. Now I craved that. I *craved* it. This felt more normal or something. It was really disappointing. Hamish banged on the table again. God, I wanted to punch his big belly out. Suddenly in my peripheral vision, Idris's cock sprang out of his pants. A white shaking bone with a slit-in red eye. Idris cupped his furry purple balls. I quickly unzipped Arne's pants. The beer had turned my tongue thick. Arne's cock was thick, sort of floppy. I wanted more beer.

"Dana, just get up!" Hamish pounded the table again.

No, nothing would make me go back to him. I wanted obliteration. The penance of cock. Idris was stroking his shaft with his fist in a frenzy. I put my slathering lips over Arne's cock head to get away from that mean red-eyed thing. More spit in my mouth. I raised up a little so my head touched the table. Arne let his legs relax. Fuck Hamish. Fuck all men. Arne's cock floundered. I spiralled and tightened my tongue. My knees bored into gum-grafted cement. Arne's cock grew. I squeezed at the thick base. The guy's pubes were weedy. His dick started to pulse. It had been three months since I'd sucked on a cock. I opened to not gag. I caught a sulphuric stench. That was Idris, jerking his cock straight at me. Hamish banged on the table repeatedly.

"Calm yourself, man," I heard Idris say.

Idris jerked under the table the way you'd stab a pig to death.

Arne felt my distraction, my occasional lolling off his cock head to watch Idris's show. So Arne cupped my head in his hands. He held my ears. It came to this, the *nice* guy leading a typical face-fuck. I got forced into his rhythm, every guy has a rhythm, and Arne had an old marching pulse: *down, down, up-down*. I started to gag. He pushed my forehead right to his patch of pubes. The second *down* was too much. Idris put his boot on my ass. Idris pointed his red-eyed whore cock at my face. I jacked my jaw wider, used suction. I didn't want to be led.

Down, down, up-down.

"I hate you, Dana," I heard from above.

Down, down, up-down.

Satan's steel toe ground between my pussy lips.

Down, down, up-down.

Everything was mealy and sweltering. I rubbed in a circle on the tip of Idris's boot. I couldn't help myself. Vulva lips mashing my clit. I kept on rubbing. Steel toe. I felt an onset of juice.

Down, down, up-up-DOWN.

Arne shot and clamped my head. I could not breathe. His cum hit my tonsils. I rubbed my cunt lips together, feeling my clit push out at the top. My pussy bore down. One hard beat on his boot. A sputter in my vagina, that's it.

Arne popped out of my mouth. I coughed and swallowed his jizz. He tried to caress my face or something, but I felt total irritation. There was Idris, wet steel toe, shaking his dick. The guy jerked at me, gunned me with his sperm in quick jolts. It was cold and sulphuric with flecks of dark cream.

I was shat on by that cock. I sat stunned and alone. Music rattled the table.

"She's done," Idris said.

I crawled out from underneath the table. I sat back down in my seat.

I took a long gulp of a third beer that the waitress brought for me. I wiped cum off my cheek. I realized I could now look Idris in the eyes. I knew Hamish would get that we were totally through. His neck had exploded in pink and brown hives.

Look, if you don't go down on a girl, I was thinking, *she is going to break up with you.*

I felt really strange. Half-drunk. Ticklish. I stood up to go.

"Don't you dare," said Hamish.

"Let her go, man," Arne said.

"That slut needs the *fire of tribulation*," Idris said.

I actually laughed. The fuck head's sulphur shots lingered on me. But the thing was, the thing was, standing up, my ass felt suddenly alive! Just like with Jay-Jay. Flames licked at my rawness. My tail *slithered* out. It was still there. Thank God. Idris had called it out to play.

Chapter 3
Locomotion

Travel light, live light, spread the light, be the light.

—*Yogi Bhajan*

I headed down towards the lake, towards the Gardiner Expressway, where cars fled the city up concrete on-ramps. I needed to walk for clarity. My feet hurt. My jaw hurt. I felt a breeze of juicy sadness. That's what Jay-Jay said about yoga—*juicy, make it juicy*. Now I think I knew what he meant. Feeling was juicy. Sadness was juicy. You pricked yourself, you wrung yourself, and something spurted out.

I didn't want to think about Hamish ever again. Bitter sex feelings are the opposite of juicy. Why hadn't I been lucky with cunnilingus in my life?

Walking towards to the expressway, I asked the universe for more.

Universe, more pussy-licking, please.

Universe, please keep this ass tail alive.

Cars blasted by me, some beeping. *Universe, rimming is part of my sexuality now.*

Empty chip bags floated in circles around a guy who was pacing under the expressway. The guy held a handmade cardboard sign: *Need Food. God Bless.* I had a fifty dollar bill in my mat bag. I walked up to the guy and, totally selfless, handed him the cash. He looked at my money, then at me, my wet pants. He rolled up the bill and shoved it in his front pocket. His bottom lip was brown, encrusted with sores.

"You got a smoke?" he said.

I shook my head no.

"Then fuck off," the guy said.

Cars raced around us in all four directions. I couldn't believe it. I'd just given him all my cash.

"Bitch like you needs a joint with a side of fat cock," the guy said, laughing.

My back started to hurt. Joint with a side of fat cock was what I'd just had. I didn't say that. Why was I always trying to make things easier for men?

The guy started laughing so hard that he began coughing. Once he started, he couldn't stop. He had to go down on one knee in the gravel. I waited and watched him. The guy had bird shit on his back. I felt pathetic and confused. When the coughing settled, I started walking up the on-ramp.

"Hey! Don't go up there! It's illegal!" the guy yelled after me, erupting into another set of hacks. "*Yoo-hoo!* Stop! You can't go there!"

It occurred to me all of a sudden that I was transparent to men, that the reason I was nice to them all the time was that they could *see* me. Hamish *knew* that I wanted a tongue in my pussy; he just wouldn't give it to me. And that guy hacking down there knew that pot was my crutch. It had been this way for two years. The only time I came from fucking anymore was when I was baked. When I smoked enough pot, my cunt could make itself come. It tightened like a clamp on Hamish's fat tummy dick, like, it could do all these things that it didn't know how to do straight. My cunt was a stoner that could tear up a cock.

"*Yoo-hoo!* You're gonna die up there!"

I walked alone at the side of the expressway, bereft. Cars veered away from my body. I touched my yoga pants. Dry. I prodded between my ass cheeks. Nothing. No more nub. What a mind fuck. I wanted to banish men who thought they knew me. Death metal was *death*. I wanted life, a yogic life!

What in the world was I supposed to *do* with my body?

Then this car beeped at me, whizzing by. It was a red KIA and it stopped on the shoulder up in front of me, hazards flashing. I ran up to it, yoga bag bouncing. All the windows were down. Inside were two guys, Asian, who seemed about my age.

"Yo, where you going like that?" the guy on the passenger side said, checking me out.

The driver wore aviator sunglasses. He had thick long black hair. "She's going to Niagara Falls," he said.

I hadn't been to Niagara Falls since I was thirteen. The back door of the KIA unlocked by remote. Somebody wearing those sunglasses, you couldn't tell what they were thinking. This was a new car; it smelled like Elmer's glue. I saw a ukulele case under the back of the driver's seat.

"Come on in," the guy on the passenger side said, encouraging. "I got a wife and a baby. We're nice bros, yeah?"

The driver was smoking a brown cigarette. He wore shiny green snakeskin-type pants. I smelled the glue of new car, and something else. Something *juicy*. So I climbed in. We took off full speed.

"You do yoga?" passenger guy said, looking at my mat bag. "My wife does it too."

Wind whipped through the driver's thick black hair. He was driving really fast. The guy from the passenger side didn't seem old enough to have a wife. It occurred to me that I needed speed.

"My wife says it helped her after the baby. You know the *mula bandha*?"

Jay-Jay said that *mula bandha* was the energy lock located between your anus and genitals. *Root lock, ladies, you got to get the key!* It occurred to me right then that Jay-Jay had triggered my *mula bandha*. My root lock was a part of my survival. My need for fucking speed! The driver smelled like cloves. He watched me in the rearview mirror.

"Peanut Pom thinks his wife's pussy is lax," the driver said.

"Fuck you, bro! Don't talk about my woman like that."

The driver smiled at me. White teeth and whipping hair. What kind of name was Peanut Pom?

"Childbirth is hard on a woman, right?" Peanut Pom turned around in his seat to face me. "But yoga makes it better. Like a whistle, right?"

Peanut Pom made a circle with his fingers and stuck his tongue through.

"He means a trampoline," the driver said.

Peanut Pom laughed. My thighs were feeling hot. The engine ran right under my ass, a motorized, moisturized trampoline.

"What's your name?" the driver asked.

Peanut Pom turned around again to look at me. "He wants to know your name."

"Yoo-hoo," I said. "My name is Yoo-hoo."

I stuck my hands down my yoga pants. My *mula bandha* was beating.

Peanut Pom's eyes got wide. "She's touching the queefer," he said.

The driver sped up, weaving between the other cars. I looked at him in the rearview mirror with both my hands shoved down my pants— one cupping my pussy, one on my clit. I wanted the driver to feel me through his chair. I felt our acceleration jack. My clit grew long. I was fucking Yoo-hoo! I could stroke it up and down. My clit was moving on its own like a little tadpole. I spread my thighs even wider. I held the driver's gaze.

"Pull over, bro," Peanut Pom said.

The driver veered into the right lane, then jerked left. He was weaving the KIA, thrilling me.

"Look at her. She's *fopping*, bro. Stop the car. Fuck."

I was rubbing my clit and humping the air, trying to feel my ass tail again. The car flew. I laughed. All of a sudden, Peanut Pom unstrapped his belt and jumped like a ten-year-old into the back seat beside me.

"Fuck, bro, I never seen a girl go at herself like this."

"Move so I can see her," the driver said. Sun beat through his thick silken hair. I could smell it. Pomade. Clove cigarettes. Peanut Pom stank like ketchup chips. I was bucking into nothing, engine under my ass. My kinky ass tail was growing again—post-Jay-Jay, post-Idris—I could feel it rise up between my smushed cheeks. I licked my lips, looking at the driver. I wanted him to keep racing us out of the city. Peanut Pom just sat there, mouth breathing on me.

"Touch my ass," I said.

"She's telling me what to do, bro, you hear?"

I smelled ketchup dusting, ass crack. Not my own ass. My own ass was sublime. I trusted that now.

Lake Ontario gleamed on my left. Farmed red pines rose on my right.

"I got this thing," I grunted at the driver. "I got this part that turns me on."

"She thinks it's a secret?" Peanut Pom said.

I had a snake in my ass with an electric little stinger.

"Shut up, man," said the driver.

"Touch her ass like she said."

I pulled out the elastic waist band of my yoga pants and scooted up. I shovelled Peanut Pom's hand right under my ass.

"Whoa," Peanut Pom said, squeezing his eyes shut. "There's something going on in here!"

Peanut Pom felt around my ass roughly. Three long black hairs curled off his chin. "She's wiggling, bro. I don't know what that is. Pull over."

The driver had only one hand on the wheel. Peanut Pom had calluses on his fingertips. I wanted the driver. I wanted *him* to touch my kinky ass. I wanted *his* white teeth to bite up my cheeks. It's true, I was *fopping*. I tried to pull down my own pants. The car raced. My pants stuck. I didn't care what this looked like.

"She's a sodomite, man!" Peanut Pom shouted. "I wanna finger her bum but there's this thing in the way."

"Let me see," said the driver.

My ass was shaking, bouncing up and down. On an upstroke, Peanut Pom yanked down my pants. I scrambled around. No one had to move me. I crawled like a dog onto my knees and wedged my hips between the front seats.

"Fuck, that's an *ass*. . ."

My butt pulsed backwards towards the driver's face. I don't know what he saw. One hand on the wheel. Did I have hairs in my ass crack? What colour was my tail? Red? Bursting purple? Satanic? *Speed*.

"Open her up," the driver said.

Peanut Pom pulled out one cheek of my ass. I was split. My cunt hung. My feet burned. I felt stubbly fingers inside me. Then the driver gripped my other ass cheek while he drove. I heard myself grunting. The driver pinched my tail. It felt black. I bit the fucking seat. My feet were trapped in my shoes. I was going to come. My toes squished together. I felt *more* than before. It was high-frequency, rapid. That driver squeezed right where I needed it; he was cutting off my blood. Little dick in my ass. *Speed* motherfucker. My feet and ass were on fire! I raged into the seat. The driver pinched me so hard at the tip that I screamed. Showering heat flooded my thighs down to my heels. I felt my ass jiggling, humping, no control. I felt my cum spraying all over the place.

"Jesus Christ," hissed Peanut Pom.

I'd showered the front seat. I'd bathed the driver's hand.

Then there was silence. Just me gnashing my teeth.

That orgasm took me outside the car.

"Go back and sit down now," the driver said. He tapped my ass. I breathed fast. I did what he said.

I was a rag doll too wide for this back seat. My tail was sticking out of my cage. Peanut Pom helped me rearrange myself. He actually buckled me in with a seatbelt. I was exhausted and my feet were sweating, and I was about to say 'thank you' but I realized Peanut Pom wouldn't even look at me as he took my tits out of my tank top. He thought he had the right to touch me just because I was on fire.

"I like those big titties," the driver said.

My head lolled away from Peanut Pom. The seat belt strap sucked me into the leathery back seat. I hated Peanut Pom and I hated myself for letting him handle my tits like they didn't belong to me.

"Such nice titties," the driver said, smiling. "Jiggling titties and fat ass."

I felt the driver mentally pinching my tail. I couldn't help it. I felt exhausted and pissed off but I had another big spasm. Involuntary. The driver and Peanut Pom laughed. My tits shook, my flesh shook, it all shook on its own.

Then the driver pulled over. It was so sudden that Peanut Pom smashed into one door. I was not done yet, coming,

I didn't know what was going on. The screeching of tires made my heart race.

"Careful, bro. I have a kid!" Peanut Pom yelled as we skidded onto the shoulder.

I really wasn't ready. The driver jumped into the back seat. He slapped my tits between the seat belt. He was on my left side. He put my left nipple deep into his mouth. He pinched hard on the other one, and my spasms didn't stop. I didn't know where I was. My pants that had been on since yoga class, Peanut Pom was finally peeling them off my knees. My pants caught on my shoes, my burgundy heels. Everything stuck. At the side of the road the driver sucked my tits between the seat belt strap, smashing my tits together into one big tit, double nipples, sucking and biting them hard. Peanut Pom tried to take off my tank top but he only got it off halfway. He left it hanging around my neck. I was strapped in at the chest, strapped from the neck. I realized that the driver had taken out his cock. I put my hand in his black hair as Peanut Pom held me in place. The driver put one hand down near my ankle straps, then he left my tits and stuck his tongue in my mouth. Fire poker. I grunted. He stroked my swelling hot feet. God, he tasted good. I sucked. The driver filled my mouth with cloves.

Cars whipped by us at the side of the road. All of a sudden I remembered that Hamish had been a good kisser. The driver stopped tonguing me. He slid his sunglasses down his nose.

"You are here with *me*," the driver said.

I nodded, but I really couldn't look him in the eyes.

"Hey, what about *me*?" Peanut Pom complained. He pulled my tank top tighter, held up my heavy tit.

The driver grabbed my chin to make me look at him. "You have to think about *me* when you're here."

A phone rang somewhere from the front seat.

My heart beat too hard. The driver's cock was purplish, engorged.

"Keep her strapped down," the driver said to Peanut Pom.

"My phone, bro." Peanut Pom seemed very far away.

I entered a fold of uncertainty. The

driver slid his mirrored sunglasses back up. He contorted his body into the space between the two front seats. His ear lobes raked along my legs. He'd wedged his head between my inner thighs. Then the driver stuck his tongue inside my pussy and he held me by the ankles. Clove semen breath. Peanut Pom pulled the tank top at my neck. I dropped into a state. The driver was a great cunt-eater. It was like his tongue could expand and contract inside me. He licked from the bottom of my vagina in tight wavy passages up to my big clit. He pushed all around the contours of my clit and then he dipped back down and worked his tongue side to side inside me. Feeling was 3-D. Trickling, waving full pistons. I came again, I couldn't help it. I didn't even have a moment of build. I came, I just came. I loved his fucking tongue inside me. My vagina spasmed and shot out one pulse of juice. The driver sucked me up like a big red balloon. I swear his jaw unhinged like a snake's and he suctioned my cunt from the pubic bone to take it all down his throat, to take me all in. I heard myself sighing. This post-orgasm orgasm was *it*. Cunt juice, big cunt buzz. My head lolled side to side.

"She's done, bro. Check her out."

"Not yet. She's got more."

The driver wiped his lips. He undid my seat belt. Then, lovingly, he removed my shoes.

"A woman should feel the ground," the driver said.

My feet freed, the driver tickled my

arches. I giggled. He fingered all my toe cracks. Eyes closed, bare feet, I felt myself rising back to him, magnetic, doing exactly what he wanted. I was drunk with cunnilingus. The phone started ringing again. Buried in my consciousness. The driver arranged me on my hands and knees, the way I was before. My back swayed. My ass pulsed. This was what it was to have a cunt. Peanut Pom silently slid like a mushroom underneath me. The driver somehow squeezed by me again into the front seat. His face was at my backside. He worked his tongue into my asshole just once. That was enough. There was lava in my tail. Peanut Pom masturbated like a slug underneath me. I never saw his little cock. My tits hung in his face.

The driver watched my ass and grabbed all my blubber.

"Lay her down on me, bro. She's fucking dripping on me, *yo*."

I started thinking about all of the men that I knew. Why didn't I ever fuck Hamish and Idris together?

The driver punched my low back. *Think about me!* I collapsed on Peanut Pom's ding. It was tiny, a jack knife. He somehow slipped it inside me. I didn't know how I was suddenly rutting a body. I pointed my toes hard.

The driver jiggled my tits to oblivion. My tail was erect. My tail wanted more.

"Condom," I squeaked.

Peanut-Pom pushed up into me and grunted. I could barely feel him.

"I'm going to finger fuck your hot ass

now," the driver said.

Something clicked. Something snapped hard between my ass cheeks.

I gaped. That was fleeting. Maybe I could gape my ass for him.

I grunted, forgetting the condom and feeling my asshole in spasm. "Fuck it," I grunted. "Fuck it right now!"

Then there was silence. Squishy rutting. My ass was everything. There was an eye in my ass and I could open and close it. I felt weirdly, wholly, sway-back relaxed. I did not care about going forward in life.

In silence, I felt his finger sliding into my tube. My back tube full of water. A tight nail scrape. The driver had his finger to the knuckle in my ass.

"Take a deep breath."

My ass clenched inside. I could not gape anymore. Gape was advertisement. There was a second digit pushing in. It didn't hurt but I was scared. I lay down on the stink of Peanut Pom's ding. I humped. The driver hooked me. He had me inside by two fingers. My asshole touched my cunt from the inside. I didn't have bones. He spit and he wedged in another one of his twigs. Finger fuck from behind. He hooked me up, tickling it, moving it around.

"Good enough," the driver said, dripping manifold sweat.

He beat his knuckles around. My insides were writhing. The phone kept on ringing. All I wanted was fuck. Then, without warning, the driver retracted his fingers. My whole body heaved.

"What is it?" I cried.

Slimy Peanut Pom scooted out of me. He answered the phone.

I felt young and scraped raw.

I turned around to look at the driver.

My throat was tight. He was sweating. Snakeskin. I wanted him close. I didn't want to cry. I needed *more*. I wasn't through!

Between the front and the back seat the driver and I started kissing again. I sucked on his tongue while I gave him dick squeezes. It felt good. He had a workaday cock. Normal size, purple head.

"Let me do you," I moaned.

I wanted it in my mouth. I wanted him to watch me suck.

Peanut Pom yelled into the phone in a language I didn't know.

I went down into the driver's lap and slid my saliva-frothed cheek on his workaday cock. I suckled the tip, I loved the head. The driver's hands pushed my shoulders. I licked around and around the dick ridge. I had lots of spit, I had lots of substance. I moved his dark shaft skin in quick up and down motions. There was life inside the body of his cock, pulsing, inner spurting, and I felt every second of it. I wanted to feel this life rise and explode. My throat enveloped his rod. The car started to shake. Clove on a burner. Yelling around. My ass tail was erect. Heat shot into my nipples. Our fire was rising. My throat clamped. One hand squeezed right there at his base, one hand jiggled and encircled his balls. Prick up, rise together. Shaft veins beat out. A cock's head that loved me was going to spray my whole throat. I kept my tongue going. God, unload it inside me. I didn't want to let it go. I never wanted to stop. But the driver kept trying to dredge me off him.

"I wanna see you," he said. "I wanna come on your face."

His taut dick's head popped out of my lips. It started spraying white cream. Drops splattered my cheeks, my nose, in my hair. I laugh-smeared. Hot jism. I slid up to his face.

"The wife wants me to come home now," Peanut Pom said.

Fuck off, I wanted to say. Me and the driver are *sharing*.

I gave the driver back some of his come. I tasted myself. Our tongues glued and flapped there. I knew I could've stayed with him, stuck. Mirrored holes in my head. We dripped sweat. I liked cum. We tried to get inside to each other.

"Come on, bro. I gotta *go*."

"Yoo-hoo, you're so hot," the driver whispered in my neck.

He was emotional. Workaday. Something propelled me. Maybe I was too hot, too bodily. This car was not my karma.

I pushed away from the driver who had done all these good things and I opened the back door with my free hand. I engaged my ass backwards and slithered out of the KIA. I was naked. Squatting, I let out a little gas.

The driver looked hurt. "This is how you say goodbye?"

Peanut Pom threw my soaking wet yoga pants out after me. "Leave her, man, leave her be."

The driver returned to the front seat. I watched him. He really had beautiful thick hair. Then he started the car with the back door still open. The two of them drove off with my kitten heels and yoga mat.

Now I was flat-footed. Now I was free.

Chapter 4
Youth

> The Gods single out at an early age
> those who are to carry consciousness
> further.
>
> —Gopi Krishna

I crawled for a while on my hands and knees, away from the highway, into the trees. My tank top hung twisted like a rope around my neck. My wet pants dragged on my back through the bush. I knew there were probably ticks in this forest. Centipedes. Wayward deer. Reluctantly, I got off the forest floor. I was a fucker. Being upright felt stiff.

I unwound my drenched tank top and slicked it back on. My pants had thinned at the crotch but I put them on too. The trees seemed to sweat, a mist fell from the sky. I walked for a while, weaving through the trunks.

Soon, the forest led out to a mud road with no divider. It curved and I walked hearing nothing but birds. Green and brown bushes grew at least eight feet tall.

Then, at the end of the road up ahead I saw a two-story brick building. It was L-shaped, alone on a gravel lot. It looked like a motel with external iron stairs. I walked towards it, thinking maybe I could get a night, take a shower. Three cars on a diagonal were parked in the lot. One was a Benz. I felt suddenly self-conscious in my yoga gear.

As I walked towards the motel, I realized that near the Benz there was a kid. She was sitting in the gravel, cross-legged, in a bikini. When the kid saw me walking towards her she put her hand over her mouth to laugh. The kid was wearing a leopard print bikini. She looked around thirteen years-old. I walked right up to her.

"Are you staying here with your family?" I asked.

The girl was all skinny legs and skinny arms, with big curly brown hair. She shook her head no. The leopard print bikini seemed at least one size too small. I realized all of a sudden that the girl had makeup on —very thick lipstick and caked-on mascara. She stayed silent, smiling, staring at me as she raked the gravel with her fingernails.

Then, a man came out of one of the rooms trailed by two girls also wearing bikinis. They looked around the same age as the girl in the parking lot, or maybe a couple of years older. The guy was in a suit. He had a large nose and a black beard, one of those see-through ones with interlocking hairs that grow just a little below the chin. Hasidic. The guy's suit jacket tightened around a lodestone gut. I got a whiff of cooking oil.

The man stared at me and clicked open his Benz by remote. The girls all had blank-looking, over-lashed eyes. If I'd had my phone I would've called 911.

"Siddiqui," the man said, sizing me up. "And you might be. . .?"

Ass mother, I thought. *Yoga slut.*

One of the girls wore a leopard print bikini exactly like the first girl's, but the third girl, standing a bit apart, wore a silver bikini. I noticed that this third girl closed her eyes.

"Let's start again," the man said to me, winking at the girl on the ground. "I am Siddiqui. And you are. . .?"

Siddiqui had yellow dog teeth. His voice had a nasal quality. The hairs of his beard were frayed at the ends.

"I don't want to tell you my name," I said quickly.

I wanted to shriek out: *My name is Yoo-hoo!*

Siddiqui put on sunglasses. What was

it with men and those mirrored sunglasses? You are trying to look at a man and he is looking at you and all you see is your fish-eye self.

"Okay, who needs a bye-bye?" Siddiqui said to the girls.

That first girl I met shot her hand up into the air and jumped up off the ground. The ponytailed second girl also raised her hand and waved it anxiously. They both jiggled around, competing for the man's attention. It seemed like they were doing what was expected, following some script. The third girl was silently swaying. Her eyes opened and closed. Her face turned light green. Siddiqui mimicked the first girl's squealing sound as she kept hopping up and down like a child. She *was* a child! The girl in the silver bikini seemed to cringe.

Abruptly, Siddiqui picked up the first squealing girl, literally scooped her up with one arm by driving it between her legs. Her crotch slid on his bicep. She was an insect compared to him. He was surprisingly strong. Then, Siddiqui stuck his tongue in her mouth. I could not believe it. This old Jewish guy in a suit was sucking face with a teen. I wished I had my phone. I would've taken a picture. I would've taken a picture for the fucking cops and not just stood there *cringing* like that girl in silver. It was a spectacle. An old man in a suit and a half-dressed teen girl. Their tongues seemed attached, as if one goose-bumped cow's tongue was throat fucking them both. There was a wet spot on Siddiqui's suit jacket. I got hypnotised by the sucking. It was half disgusting, half magical.

"Go down," said Siddiqui.

The girl slid off his arm like she was at the playground.

"Me next! Me next!" squealed the second ponytailed girl as she sashayed up to Siddiqui.

What sort of playground was this? Was I really just going to stand there and watch a second slippery sacrifice?

"Looky-look," Siddiqui said, nodding at something behind me.

My head felt skeletal, bugged. I turned around. That girl Siddiqui had just tongued had her hand shoved down her too-tight bathing suit bottoms. She was writhing around like a ribbon, masturbating. It looked like she was actually going to come. Her mouth was a fake O, her eyes were squeezed shut, and her hand kept opening and closing through the spandex panties.

"Go on," Siddiqui said to the second girl, tapping her bum. "We have a visitor."

The second girl obediently skipped up to the gyrating first girl. They were acting like strippers, fully aware. The second girl sank down to her knees in the gravel and yanked the first girl's bikini bottom down. The first girl was yipping now, high-pitched, while frigging. She had a big hairy pussy. That shocked me. Or maybe that was good. I watched the second girl part the first girl's pussy lips with her fingers. It was so clear that she'd done this before. She was parting it like that and shifting her body to the side so we could see. It made me sick. The second girl's tongue stuck out and wriggled at the first girl's black thatch. The first girl held the second girl's ponytail and jerked her in the air. They both knew exactly what to do.

I realized that this was a sex show, a fake teen-girl sex show *for me*, but I could not move or do a thing. I felt sex in my eyes, tingling behind my eye sockets. My throat felt like a piece of rock. The rest of my body was gone. My ass tail shriveled. And as the first girl started humping the second girl's ponytailed head, I finally tore my buzz eyes away.

"Go down, girls, go down," hissed Siddiqui behind me.

I tried to hold the third girl's gaze and keep my eyes away from the sight.

But the second girl was now maneuvering herself to the ground. In my peripheral vision: the second girl in the leopard print bikini lay flat on her back, smashing her ponytail in the gravel. I *had* to look. They were both facing me: mouths open, tongues out. The first girl hovered in a squat over the second girl's tongue. She looked innocent and powerful with that thatch. The second girl, the one on her back, reached her skinny arms up. Charged air hit my throat. My whole face was beating. They were doing this for me.

"My prize cunts," Siddiqui whispered behind me.

"Stop it," I shot back.

I was glued to them, crouching down, eyeballs like crack.

"Girls, time for bed," Siddiqui snapped.

I felt my stuck tears. The girls jolted up, giggling. A weak sunset blanched us in sickly pink light.

"You want to come inside?" Siddiqui asked. He had taken off his suit jacket. His armpits were soaked.

The two bikinied girls skipped off holding hands into one of the rooms.

"No, no. I'll be going." Now I was the one with the nasal sound.

My neck creaked. I started to hobble in the gravel. My yoga pants were drooping. I needed sunglasses to deflect this bad light.

"Don't go."

The third girl. She *spoke*. I stopped. She looked angry. Her long brown hair hung limp; it hid all its knots. I looked at her and she looked at the ground, as if she hadn't just asked me to stay. Her breasts were bigger than the others'. Her mouth was downturned. Pubic hair curled out of her silver spandex bikini bottom.

"Tamara doesn't ever join the fun," Siddiqui snorted. "Cold Fish Tamara, we call her. She gets all our rape culture customers because she's a cold fish."

I wanted to vomit in that parking lot. Vomit under the parachute of rape.

I started to feel a buzzing back in my legs. I started to feel my gut again. I felt my pelvis: my pubic bone, my tailbone, and a hollow nerve channel in between. Tamara had this amorphous, almost puffy body: fidgety and alien. Okay, I realized that Tamara was dissociated and I had been *woke*. I was not a rape culture man. God, I felt guilty. Twigged. I had to *do* something.

I thought: I could make this cold fish come.

I couldn't help those two girls but I could help *her*.

Jay-Jay woke me up at the root. I had a stinger in my ass.

Tamara. I said her name in my head. I had sexual knowledge. It was meant to be shared.

"As long as you let me in with you," Siddiqui whispered, watching me think, "you two can have a room tonight."

I stared at Tamara, trying to send her messages of heat. Tamara finally looked back up at me: consent.

"But you have no rights to the footage," Siddiqui added.

At that moment I did not care about my rights. There was a human being here that I needed to help. This was not about my rights.

"Come-come," Siddiqui said.

Tamara moved first. She shuffled. I followed her as she followed Siddiqui around to the back of the building. There was a rust-colored dumpster, a junked car, piles of black garbage bags. The sky descended into darkness without stars.

Siddiqui unlocked a door with a long golden handle. "This is our special lovers' lookout room," he said.

Siddiqui walked in first, then Tamara. Her back hunched, her pelvis drooped. I hated her bikini. I knew that she'd had the shit kicked out of her in life.

Inside the room, the air was musty,

the light dim. I told myself to be strong. Siddiqui turned on a rose-shaded pottery lamp by the bed. The walls seemed like plywood. Spider webs plugged up the corners. From the oversized picture window you could see floodlights in the distance, surrounding Niagara Falls — one big teeming hole in the earth.

Tamara hung back near the closet. Her nipples were hard. My heart beat too fast.

Siddiqui cleared his throat on purpose. I told myself that whatever happened, he would not direct this at all.

"Come over here," I said, looking at Tamara. I stood at the base of the king-size bed. It had pink quilted pillows. A mothball dump.

Tamara stood there, stiff and unmoving.

I remembered Jay-Jay telling us about the heart center. *Anahata*, he said, punching his own chest. *This heart is unhurt, unstruck, unbeaten.* He made us beat our own chests and chant that with him. Unhurt, *punch*, unstruck, *punch*, unbeaten, *punch punch*.

"My name is Yoo-hoo," I said, looking at Tamara and taking a deep breath right into the middle of my chest.

Siddiqui had moved around towards the TV.

"I'm glad you told me not to go," I said.

Tamara finally looked at me straight, unblinking. I felt a beating speed in my throat. I realized I had speed inside me. I didn't need external speed. Tamara was silent but steady.

She had eyes like a deer's. I knew she wasn't going to move any closer to me though, so I went up to her and just took her by the hand. It was an ice-covered branch.

"You're *okay*," I said, squeezing.

Tamara said nothing. Her reticence was turning me on. I wanted to say that I knew that she could move. I wanted to say she had beautiful boobs. Her tits touched each other in the middle of her bikini. I wanted to light her fingernails on fire. I wanted to find her hidden ass tail.

"I'm okay," Tamara muttered, looking back down.

I led her to the edge of the bed. Tamara sat down on her own. Her tits were rising up and down.

"I'm going to take off your bikini now," I whispered.

Tamara nodded yes. Her hair fell into her face. She crossed her ankles. There were dark, flat hairs on her legs.

"Wah, this is good," Siddiqui said from somewhere.

"I want to see your whole body, okay?" I swallowed. My throat was swelling. I felt my heart jumping around.

Tamara nodded and closed her eyes.

"No," I ordered. "Don't close your eyes."

"I have to," she whispered.

"Why?"

"When I close my eyes," Tamara said, "I like what I see on the screen."

I wanted her to watch me seduce her. I didn't want her to have her own film.

Tamara's eyes brimmed with tears. "I'll do everything else that you ask me, okay?"

"She doesn't need to do anything you ask her," Siddiqui panted.

Please, Tamara, I thought as I took down her panties. *Men are gonna want to try to crucify you, take advantage of you, stuff their cocks in your face. You gotta see that stuff coming!*

Tamara, shut-eyed, with tear-splattered cheeks, let me fully wiggle off her panties. I wanted to keep her tits jiggling in the top. I wanted to keep her pliant, heating up. I hated that Siddiqui was watching. I thought of all the times when I didn't open my eyes.

"You're okay," I assured her.

I pushed her knees open. My first

glimpse of her pussy. She had thick vulva lips that stuck shut and flat, dark brown pubic hairs like mismatched pine needles. I pushed Tamara back onto the bed. She didn't expect me to do that. Because she did not open her eyes.

All at once I realized where I was. It was like for a second I flew up to the ceiling and looked down, bird's-eye. I was in a *brothel*. What I also realized was that I had a teenager, a cold fish, all to myself; a teenager who was opening for me. I felt *experienced*. I wanted to take my time. I landed back in my body. Things were coming full circle. I felt this roiling surge of energy. Tamara writhed and mewled as I pressed on her inner thighs. I felt this sudden rush of superhuman strength. I flipped Tamara like a wrestler onto her belly. Her ass was fleshy and I started squeezing it, hard, then I pulled her cheeks apart. Tamara started pushing her pussy into the bed. She *liked* it hard. I heard Siddiqui heave-panting behind us. I kneaded Tamara's ass cheeks in a circle, pressing them together and splitting them apart. Her hips kept gyrating into the mattress. We were working together. I felt powerful. I put one knee on the back of her thigh, pinning her. Tamara was writhing around and moaning. She was signalling to me how she dug my pressure, my containment, while she pretended to struggle. Her tits spread out to the sides underneath her. I always liked it when a guy felt my tits from the side. So I did that, leaving her ass for a second but not letting up on her legs. I squeezed her tits from the side and rubbed them up to her armpits. I pinched her flesh to get underneath. Tamara's bum rose off the bed. Her back was so sway. She was showing off her puss with all the little spider hairs.

"Put your finger in," I said. That's what I wanted to see.

Tamara kept bumping her ass up into the air. I moved my free hand up near her neck and clamped down for a moment.

"You said you would do whatever I wanted."

"Okay," she moaned into the mattress.

Tamara, ass shaking, eyes closed, in her own private realm, stuck one chicken finger up her thick cunt. That transition. *Insertion*. I felt it in myself. Unmoored, above, my thighs flooded with heat.

"Move it," I said.

Tamara's hair plastered her eyes-squeezed-shut face.

"Come on, we wanna see you finger yourself."

I was including Siddiqui. I was including the world.

Tamara's pussy was hungry. It sucked another bubbling finger.

"We love watching you finger fuck yourself."

"You do?" Tamara mumbled.

I responded by butting myself up against her ass. She suddenly laughed. She could feel me: female, erect and in charge. Tamara finally peeked one eye open. She tried to look back at me with her slitty fingers coated. I didn't have to tell her to waggle in a third. Tamara was the third girl, three digits up her slick puss.

"Yeah, it's big, the world's so big. . ."

Tamara's free hand was slapping her clit. Her eyes wide. This was *fopping*. Asses heaving up and down.

I was just getting into all of the action, feeling my tail start to push out, when all of a sudden Tamara's three fingers shot out of her crack. Juice lathered her knuckles, shiny fingernails.

I released my pressure on Tamara's upper back and slapped her ass cheek so hard that she bucked.

"I'm sorry," Tamara moaned. "Yoo-hoo, I couldn't help it."

I slapped Tamara's cheeks at least ten more times. I felt really angry. I wasn't even sure why. I made these red patches all over her ass. I'd been building into something, building into her ass, and she came on her own! She came way too fast! I was just getting started and the girl fucking came! It was bullshit. It occurred to me at that moment that maybe they were using me, Tamara and Siddiqui. They were just using my knowledge to get at each other. . .

"Yoo-hoo, *please*," Tamara cried.

I did not let Tamara recover. I did not let her turn over. In that moment, I had no more compassion for her. I used both my hands and grabbed each of her ass cheeks, like I started to before, but this time, ferocious. I remembered Jay-Jay, how he split my ass open with no mercy, how he exposed my bud pucker to make the ass tail. Everything blurred. I split Tamara open. *Hands and knees, bitch. I'm transforming you.* Tamara was frantic, mewling. Inside of her asshole was a sea horse with finlike, fanned-out bone splints. I spit in her asshole. I gave her some lube. I could feel all my hard strength, my tail really pushing out. I wanted my pants down, my tits out. I wanted to be seen from behind. I wanted to expose my own ass as I fucked up in hers. I pulled down my pants. I felt the air thinning. There was an asshole behind me who grunted at my fat ass. Tails were human. There was energy inside.

"Yoo-hoo, *mmmm*, *mama*, it hurts."

She had a wild red ass and I spit on it again. I knew I could make her feel what I felt. My own ass started to open and shake. I was dancing it, showing it. Yes. I felt gape. *Agape.* I felt vines slither out.

My bud to the sun, which was eyes, total yes, the ass moved by itself. I kept splitting her ass flesh, going in to the poker, wanting to eat it and suck it until we were both burning up, alive.

"Ooooh, Yoo-hoo, I think I'm going to—"

I was Jay-Jay supreme. I poked my tongue in her. It smelled like seaweed. My tail flickered long. A devil's tail, an antennae of sex, it knew how to fork and fuck sharply for me. I was making a new woman feel her own ass. Rimming it to tease out her bumps, penetration to feed her darkest sparks. It was hot in her asshole. I felt a light crack in mine.

"That's good, girls, that's good, that looks really good. . ."

Tamara sucked on her fingers. My

whole mouth was inside of her ass. I heard her moaning *no* but I knew she didn't mean *no*. Her seahorse was kissing me, I was eliciting tail. She was wet from the cunt and it flooded everywhere. I had all her cunt froth for more rimming, more licking, my tongue up her stint hole to pull out her insides. It occurred to me to double down. Really take her down, take her inside. I slid my fingers up her pussy. The pulsations of life. Tamara passed the vibrations back to me. We generated this fucking. My asshole gaped more naturally than it ever had before. For one second I wished Siddiqui would pole me while I was inside her ass. I wished I could fuck Tamara with a cock. A fake cock, a real cock. I wished I could hold her down by the back and, just like she was, ass displayed, back swayed, put my fat cock like a maypole inside her. Inside all her holes, stuff her cunt and her ass and say, *I made you come, bitch. You've been depriving everyone.*

"Oooh, Yoo-hoo, God, Yoo-hoo, *God, I love you, Yoo-hoo!*"

My fingers scooped in and out of this pussy, my thumb on this clit, my face in this ass, I licked this new asshole and prodded it with circles. I pulled out a tail, electrical jolts.

Tamara went feral. One man-sized gush. Her bum hit my cheeks. *Everything* spasmed. Her pussy tightened on my fingers. Her ass clutched at my tongue. She was sucking her fingers and fucking my face with her butt and I couldn't help myself because she was coming, releasing, but still I didn't pull back. I poked my tongue higher up her tight ass, all those starry stints, I kept going like a ramrod right into her coming. She pulsed on me, came on me, flooding me with life. I reached around to hold her tits. She was mine. She was mine. The cold fish was all mine.

Tamara collapsed on the king-size bed. I slid up her back. She lay on her belly and I lay on top, burying my wet face in the dip of her neck. Her sour sop hair was all over me. I think she was crying. I was crying. We writhed around like that, feeling the velvety cilia vibrations of each other.

Then we both got a cold jab. Siddiqui jizzed out. He was standing over us and he aimed at her lips. It was rough. Tamara jerked. Siddiqui had a lot of come. Tamara licked her cum-strung lips from habit, or something. She slurped it all up. I pulled away. It was as if she truly liked his goopy geezer jizz! *I* was the one who had just made her come! I rolled off Tamara's back. I wanted to go.

Tamara looked at me with sad eyes as I pulled up my pants. I wished my cunt wasn't so sopping, so swollen.

I really wanted to leave. Siddiqui was coming to take her. I felt totally exhausted by the two of them.

But Tamara covered herself with the wet pink bedspread and she said: "I don't want to work here anymore."

Siddiqui rubbed the sweat off his temples. He stood by Tamara at the side of the bed. The picture window behind him revealed clusters of grimy fingerprints. Siddiqui put his hand under Tamara's chin and forced her to look up.

The phone was in my reach. I could call 911.

"*Siddi*, please," hissed Tamara. "Let me go with her!"

Tamara's plea was the crux of kept-in behaviour, years and years of survival sex.

"You are brainwashed, *maidele*, that's the thing."

Siddiqui did not let go of Tamara. But Tamara cranked her neck hard and broke away from him. It was as if she flew towards me. The walls buckled. Tamara was clammy and shaking and she burrowed like a child into my chest. All I could do was hold her tight.

Siddiqui looked at us, raking his chain beard.

"She'll be back," he said. Then he left.

Chapter 5
Purge

> So in the center of the heart is a furnace. Either it can cook for you or it can burn down your house and there is nothing in between.
>
> —*Yogi Bhajan*

Shaking and naked, Tamara tore the bedspread from the bed. She ripped off the stained mattress cover and whipped all the pink quilted pillows around. Dirty gray feathers shot through the air.

"I want to tear stuff up, Yoo-hoo."

Tamara's eyes bulged. Her tits hung. Her hair was plastered back with sweat. She jumped up onto the dirty bare mattress and kicked the headboard again and again. The whole room rattled. Ceiling plaster rained down. Tamara bared her teeth and kicked till the headboard straight cracked. Then she jumped up and down, reaching for the crystal light fixture. Tamara clamped onto a hanging strand and gave the thing a yank. The whole ceiling rattled. A dust storm of plaster surrounded her head. Tamara flung the plastic chandelier. It hit the window like a squid.

I was totally mesmerized.

Tamara squatted chicken-thighed on the dirty grey mattress. She stared at me, grinning. She started to piss. Her urine wobbled like a laser. She burned a molten hole through the bed. My breath sped. I instinctively pulled down my pants too. Tamara perched above me. Her release was contagious. I squatted and pissed on the rust colored carpet. There was so much release. The room steamed with our hot yellow piss. It felt good in my pussy. It made my thighs shake.

Tamara jiggled on the wet bed above me. Her tits looked alive. All of a sudden, as I finished pissing, Tamara leaped over my head. In one fell, she ripped a painting off the wall. She stomped on it, pierced it. I started to laugh. Then she whipped the whole frame at the picture window. The frame split in half. Tamara bolted to the bathroom, breathing loudly.

I heard a thud and then glass shattering. Tamara emerged brandishing a plastic blow dryer over her head.

"I wanna shove this up his ass! You think this fits up his ass?"

The corkscrewing, hanging black cord of the blow dryer reminded me of the tail in my ass. Tamara turned in a circle, cackling, waving the dryer like a gun. It was as if that hog tail cord in my ass was a part of my former light self. Things were serious now. Dark.

"C'mon, you think this fits up his ass? I wanna tear up his ass. . ."

I realized that one of Tamara's front teeth was cracked.

"I don't think it'll fit," I said gently.

Tamara suddenly hurled the hair dryer at the picture window. She was angry. The thing shattered and fell on the ruins of the chandelier.

Tamara found her bikini at the foot of the bed. I smelled pussy. Tamara ripped opened all the dresser drawers. She threw out boxes of condoms and rolls of duct tape. Then she found matches. I smelled fresh ass. Tamara lit a match and tossed it at the window. It fizzled and bounced off onto the lump of bedding on the floor.

"Let's go," I said, feeling tightness in my throat.

Tamara struck and tossed match after match. "What're you so scared of, Yoo-hoo?"

Tamara saw through me and my bravado. Maybe this was the difference between us: the ability to handle fear.

Tamara walked up to me with a crooked smile, slinging on her bikini top.

She had all this heat coming off her, like bright orange heater box waves. She was right up in my face. The pile had lit. The blow dryer, the painting, and the chandelier were on fire.

"I don't want you to get hurt," I said, not able to move towards the door.

The dirty mattress cover sparked.

"Yoo-hoo, I'm already hurt."

Toxic flames grew behind us. Tamara stuck her tongue in my mouth. I sucked it. I sucked it so hard. She pushed her tits up against me. We mashed tits. We sweated. She grabbed the flesh of my ass, made it shake furiously. I felt her hot pussy grind up into mine. And the room burned itself. Circus circle of fire. We licked lips on the move. We fought each other backwards out the door, into the night air. Then we scuttled along the side of the motel. I didn't know what was next. It was pitch black in the lot. I realized immediately that Siddiqui's Benz was not there.

"Where did he go?" I croaked, still feeling her tongue.

Tamara left me and ran up to the one car left in the lot — a Fiat. She punched her fist down hard into the windshield. One shot smashed it up. Fucking life force destruction. An alarm rang out. I panicked.

"Follow me, Yoo-hoo!" Tamara screamed.

I scrambled, on autopilot, as Tamara moved stealthily along the row of motel doors, banging her hips in to try and break them down. The Fiat's alarm pierced the air. Black smoke rose from the back of the building.

I was bathed in a shiny cold sweat. Tamara pulled me inside a banged open door.

"Buck up, Yoo-hoo," she said. She could feel me shaking all over.

In the dim, creepy light, a lump of bodies lay there on the bed. Egg smell, nasal wheeze. Tamara lit a fresh match. We stood there for a second watching the rise and fall of the lump. Then Tamara burnt her finger on the flame. She cursed and lit another match. She held it up.

"Wake up," she hissed.

Tamara violently tore off the covers. The first girl and the second girl slept curled up together. They mewled and they shivered, entwined in spandex.

Tamara looked up at me, livid. "Yoo-hoo, you gotta help me. Come on!"

I came to life. Freaked out by the fire. Her anger. Girls need to help each other out to stay alive. I started kicking the bed with my bare feet. I realized exactly what Tamara was just about to do.

The girls kept curling into each other like slugs.

"Wake up!" I screamed. This was a nightmare.

Tamara pitched the final match. The girls shrieked. I yanked their arms and legs out. The bed burned like a birthday cake.

"Run!" Tamara yelled at the girls.

The girls were at the door. They looked like chickens, saucer-eyed.

"Yoo-hoo, help me burn this place down!"

Tamara threw me a fresh pack of

matches from the night table. I lit them one by one, like her. We created more fire. Another room of burning sheets. Divination. Liquidation. The first girl and the second girl disappeared through the parking lot.

"Let's get out now!" I yelled.

I could barely see Tamara through the thick smoke. I tripped backwards, gulping air.

When I re-emerged in the parking lot, a man in a short white towel was fumbling at the front door of his punched-in Fiat. The car alarm kept whinnying. The man was trying to stop it. I looked around for Tamara, who finally shot out of the burning room with a blow dryer over her head. The car alarm would not stop. The man stared at us in shock.

"What?" Tamara shrieked. "You want this poker up your bum-hole?"

The man, soaked with sweat, clutched his phone and took our picture.

"Let's go!" I screamed.

I grabbed Tamara's hand. The man clicked shots. She would not let go of the blow dryer. I had to yank her away by the cord.

"I'm going to blow this poker up his sphincter, Yoo-hoo!"

As I pulled Tamara raving into the forest, the motel erupted in flames. The whole edifice collapsed in on itself.

Chapter 6
Gorge

In our spiritual rebirth we are like puppies born in a sack. The teacher is like the mother who must eat the sack to free the puppy so that it can grow.

—*Swami Rudrananda*

The night air was humid along the dirt road. My singed yoga clothes felt like wrinkled grape skins. I was relieved to be away from the fire. But I had this sneaking, wrecked feeling of being chased while walking free. The tree trunks glistened in sequence. My sweat felt like taffy. The night birds sang: grating, high-pitched.

"Listen," whispered Tamara, skittish.

Sirens sounded far off, multiple fire alarms.

We walked quickly, in silence. Tamara sprang ahead of me, then she lagged behind. Blue floodlights shone up ahead through the trees. The dirt road opened onto an outpost of concrete. The falls were right there, pounding, spewing pale blue steam.

"Siddiqui knows where I go," Tamara whispered. "He knows what we did."

The floodlights droned. They surrounded the falls. Tamara's stress was contagious. I scanned both ways for the Benz while Tamara careened across the road holding the blow dryer like a gun. I followed her but I thought: I cannot go down with this ship.

Tamara pitched up to the limp rope barriers. The concrete got foam-like under my feet.

"Niagara is the locus of *yoni* violence," Tamara hissed.

I stood behind her, looking at the falls. I felt these magnetic filaments in the air. I tried to take a deep breath. But all I felt was her stress.

"Let's go down," I suggested weakly, trying to change the toxic energy. "Let's have a private waterfall show."

Tamara didn't even look at me. "*You* go, Yoo-hoo. I have work to do up here."

I didn't understand why she was so dismissive. Then Tamara crouched over, going for something on the ground. It was a half-eaten hot dog with teeth marks inside it. I tried to grab Tamara's palsying hand but she pushed me away.

You are brainwashed, maidele, that's the thing.

A blast of cold, rotten air hit my nose. "Please!" I cried.

I just wanted her to stop. But Tamara grabbed the dirty hot dog and she put it in her mouth. I totally freaked out. I charged and I ran. I jumped the limp ropes to a path going downward, straight down into Niagara Falls. I actually thought she would follow. I sent out my life force, my ass jets. I really wanted her to follow me.

"Tamara!" I screamed into the fog.

But Tamara didn't follow. She was up

there on land sucking some half-eaten wiener, dangling a cord. I could not yank her out of this violence. Maybe my life force was really fucking weak. The falls foamed and pounded. I felt a chasm of shame. I thought: you cannot make a fool or a goddess follow you.

"Tamara," I whimpered as the pathway started to get very steep.

Slick mud covered the thin wooden slats. All around me was cliff face supporting the falls. The path was pockmarked with half-uprooted trunks.

Tamara.

I descended. The air thinned; it hurt to breathe in. It occurred to me in this freezing cold froth that maybe Tamara was right, maybe this sucking wet hole in the earth was the crux of *yoni* violence.

Cunts were being impounded. Waters were hemmed in by concrete. Birth control equals death. How the fuck did men get away with this violence?

I felt like I was having an asthma attack. My nostrils tightened. My skull had gone dark. Pain in my temples bubbled to the surface like blisters. *Tamara*. I thought, I will never see her again.

I remembered Jay-Jay telling us in yoga how to make it through pain. He said, *breathe, ladies, breathe! Breathe into the pain.* He said, *You are like warriors staring out at the horizon. You've got to be ready for anything.* But the horizon blurred. And the falls stormed around me a hundred feet tall. I used to be on a spiritual path. Now I'd fucked in front of a *pedophile*. I'd left my traumatized sister at the precipice.

I was not breathing right. My clothes were soaked through with sludge. Black mushrooms grew between half-yanked-out tree roots. Out of the range of floodlights, I slipped.

Then I finally saw something up ahead through the haze. It looked like a man with a fishing pole; a man crouched into the crook of a rock. He had a bucket beside him. I waved my arms in the air. All of my fingers and toes had gone numb.

"Yoo-hoo!" I screamed. "Yoo-hoo! Yoo-hoo!"

The man first heard me, then he saw me.

"Yoo-hoo!" I jumped up and down, thought I was going to faint. The gorge swirled around me in foamy white pox.

"I can't breathe," I yelled, hyperventilating.

The man skipped over rocks towards me with his fishing rod. Steam rose off of his rain-hat and army pants. I held on to a tree root as he slip-sped to me, shaking off sludge, a drenched black cat. I thought he was a fireman, a fisherman, a thief. The guy took me in calmly. He scanned me, head, tits, and feet. I was wheezing, high-yipping in the terrible fog. The man had a panther-like, dark brown sculpted face.

"I can't breathe," I repeated.

The man put a hand on my shoulder, slipping a finger under my strap. "You gotta use your gills down here," he shouted at me over the noise.

Tears poured out of my eye sockets. My throat puffed. I tried to feel gills.

"I'm Morris," the man yelled. He didn't take his hand off my shoulder. "You don't need to freak out."

But my heart was really speeding. I was thinking about Tamara and the hot dog, Tamara and the fire, spitting out cum strings, beating heart pain.

Morris's T-shirt, plastered to his chest, showed me the pointed domes of his nipples. He had cold white bubbles hanging off his dark black chin hairs. He had a paunch. Bright white teeth. Fish tang. Five feet.

This guy didn't want to know my name. But his presence helped me remember how to breathe. I felt fresh slits open out all over me.

I held on to Morris's fishing rod as we scaled the sludgy brown underside of the falls. It felt like we were scaling a sphere. An inverted sphere, the texture of cervix. I took in tiny weep breaths. We turned a precarious corner. My bare feet slid on the ice cold silt. My fingers kept slipping off his rod.

"The American side!" Morris yelled backwards at me.

I breathed through my gills as I tried to get a better hold on Morris's pole. But my fingers kept slipping as we made these sharp semi-circles. Morris picked up a hook full of fish from some cranny; the fish jerked around like charms near his waist. Stripes of dawn broke the sky. Steam infected the air. The earth, it seemed, was a tortoise shell.

Suddenly Morris dipped his head under a massive offshoot waterfall. He disappeared behind the pounding gray screen. His rod tugged me to follow. It slipped. I let go. I could've split; I was wavering, destabilized. But I took a deep breath, slits opened, and forged through the wall of water. The top of my head cracked. Water pounded. I stayed there too long. Felt the pummelling of my diadem.

Om.

I touched my cold open head in the sudden heat of the other side. I wobbled around in some burnt orange enclosure. My chin bobbed. My head ached. There were hooks and cast iron pots on the walls. Morris stood inside warming his hands by a fire.

"Hey," I breathed, dizzy. "I feel really high."

Morris had tight black hair in a kind of medieval, balding-pattern ring around his ears. I noticed a bruise in the middle of his brow.

"Are you okay?" I asked, suddenly giggling, spinning towards the sunken fire.

It was so hot in the cave. Hysteria. That pummelling, thousand-eyed waterfall had pierced my crown *chakra*! That bruise on his forehead was a dent, a bullet mark.

"I pray a lot," said Morris, rubbing his forehead in a circle.

In this cave there were papers stuck to the walls beside the pots. The papers were filled with cursive writing, ink blots.

Flames rose out of oil in tiny craters in the walls. Was I back in caveman times? I walked right up to his chest at the hearth. We were the same height. I was still feeling so weird, feeling see-through, feeling *everything*. It was like my forehead had just been dented like his. Colors and dots swirled in front of Morris's body, colors I'd never seen before: magenta with green flecks, dusk pear, foamy beige. A glow emanated from the top of Morris's head.

"Morris," I whispered. "Are you some kind of witch?"

Morris smiled. I swatted the orbs in the air near him.

"I wanna fuck," I said.

Pings shot up my spine. Our skulls were joined in one bubble. My gonads got hot.

"I've been wearing these rags for a really long time!" My voice crackled, ticklish and amplified. Breathing felt strange.

I just wanted to lick his witchy nipples, feel his witchy cock, burn my witchy clothes in the fire.

Morris smiled down at me. A purplish-brown orb from his forehead descended and touched me. It was so amazing. I mean, I'd never had the feeling before of 'loving myself.' But I think this was it. I felt like a spinning top, standing still. Ticklish pink cunt juice trickled down my thighs.

"I was about your age," Morris said, smiling at me, "when I met this girl. . . She was something like you."

"I was in Cairo. You know, there's these markets everywhere... And I saw the pyramids, the Sphinx, I took a camel into the desert... I was a virgin in Cairo, on tour, okay, you get that? My father had always been very strict. He told me, you don't take the first girl your dick head gets hard for. You take the woman you're serious on and you love her for life."

I felt this instinct to grab my ass and split it. Love it for life.

"So I believed my old man, right, for *eighteen years*, and I'm fighting for my country, right, and I was too old not to have *knowledge*. I knew that. I felt that. So my buddies, you know, they don't understand... Well, they were on a mission, too. *We* were on a mission. And in Egypt they go to me, *Moe, you don't need to see her face in this land."*

My cunt and my asshole were intractable feminine features of me.

"I wanted one girl that I saw in the market, in her family stall. She had bells and whistles, right? Kohl on her eyes. Her mother stirred this big pot of stew. And her daddy took my money. He knew we were army. Her own daddy led me behind the thick curtains, and the girl, she just lay there on the cot watching black and white TV."

Morris had a pack of cigarettes in his army pants. He put one between his lips. "I get a good deal on hydroponic from my native brothers in Buffalo," he said, holding out a fresh hand-rolled cigarette for me.

Morris leaned down and lit his cig in

the fire. I followed his lead. I was now naked in his cave, partaking.

"This girl, okay, she had fabric on her face, she had Kohl on her eyes, but she showed me her face. My buddies were *wrong*. I memorized this girl's face. Her green eyes so big, right, with slits and black markings, nose fleshy at the tip, phalanges smooth. She had a little waist I could hold with both hands, she had pigeon skin, she was a breasty one. I visited her on that cot in the market behind the curtain for seven nights, every night, because it turns out that she was my spiritual wife and I was her spiritual husband," Morris said.

Our herbal blue smoke filled the cave. I wondered if this was the first spiritual man that I'd ever met.

"This girl on the cot, okay, she showed me what a *female* could do. I mean her sexual work, like, in tandem with her mouth, she was like Mata Hari, okay. I know that's a stereotype, but this girl was Middle Eastern, born in the north of Africa, and she moved right, her birthright, she knew what to do—how to shake her flesh, squeeze inside, she showed me exactly what a female body could do. In that market, behind the curtain, she sat on me, right, I mean first on my chest, she smothered me, slicked me down tight with her body and kept me under her power without my full breath. That girl with the green eyes enfolded me, right, and she made me know her pussy first, I tasted it, fingered it, fucked it with my tongue, and then later, okay, like, on the third day, she took my dick in her hands, she spurted oil from her mouth, she spurted oil from her pussy, just thinking about it makes my dick hard, like, this girl could clap her pussy open and clamp it down like a vise. I'm telling you, I've never told anyone this, I didn't know a girl's insides could have all that grip muscle... Once she took me in her bottom, it was a part of her whole, like, she was fat shaking, oil spurting, squeezing my dick. My old man did not know that there's this female orgasmic magnetism, *mama*. A spiritual wife knows how to control her insides. I did not ever want to leave this girl on the cot."

"So why did you leave her?" I asked, bathed in a coil of smoke.

Morris finished his cigarette and

tossed it onto the hearth.

"Because," he said, "she told me to."

Colors rained down from the ceiling of the witch. I was suddenly dizzy. Morris went silent and so did I. The walls glistened. My life grew. Then Morris opened his mouth and showed me his tongue. It was long and purple; it had a silver stud through it.

"You're the first girl who found me this deep in the earth," Morris said. "You're a special one, eh?"

I nodded yes. I was stoned. I was special.

Fluorescent pink dots flitted in front of my face. I thought about Tamara. Her love, her cord. The purple orb hung over Morris's head like a lampshade.

"Come on over, *mama*," Morris

said.

He lay down on the damp floor of his cave. Smoke emerged from his throat. Morris unzipped his pants. His penis stood up through the silver teeth. He had a purple-black tusk. A rod mystical. My nipples were nails.

"You're real hot, *mama*. I feel you like a furnace everywhere."

I had slits. I had gills. Morris held the base of his cock. It emanated sparks that lit the slits up inside me. I pictured his spiritual wife behind a screen. I closed my eyes and saw Tamara, her deep starfish ass.

"Come and sit your fine ass on me, *mama*. You've been splitting it over there for a while..."

I wiggled, ecstatic, over to Morris.

I stepped over his face. I shook all my flesh. Then I turned and faced his cock so he could see me full bottom. The spiritual wife shares her knowledge of sex. She told me to squat. She said, *men need display*. I was leaking my ticklish pink pussy juice. It was smeared on my thighs. I held my tits up. I bounced once down onto Morris's mouth. His pierced tongue touched my ass crack. Delectation. Fuck! My ass tail had an erection like his. I watched Morris's cock tremble from side to side. Everything moved in slow motion. Blood pulsed. Open slits. If sex was like this, I could stop *yoni* violence. I wanted to tell Tamara, we could stop *yoni* hate. Suddenly, I plunged down. I surrendered control. My doggy ass tail mashed into Morris's throat. I heard him gagging and he pulled me *more* onto him. There was a warrior at my back, tongue fucking me. The Warrior of Niagara Falls. He took what I had for him. Doggy bum. Clit lips. I wanted this to go on forever, ass to face smash, and I wanted to show Morris how hot and tight I was everywhere. I wanted to show him what *Yoo-hoo* could do: jiggle every inch of her flesh, take him in every single suck hole, even her skull rush diadem.

I had subsumed monstrosity as my *karma*. I had subsumed every weeping wacked *yoni* inside me.

I shifted up off of Morris's jaw-wide panther head. I squeezed his lacquered cock and gave it a throat plunge. But one plunge of this mystical rod was not enough. I kept sucking and throating and pledging my love. Was it love? Did I have to pledge love?

I was ready for ass sex with a cock in my mouth.

The cave was burning full of oils: fish, clove, clementine.

I scrambled onto all fours. I shook my ass, clapped it. Morris finally shed his army pants. His cock stuck straight out like a cross from a bush.

"That looks good, *mama*, yasss."

My undulations were showing. There was cock everywhere. Tails grow out of pleasure machines. Morris wanted to look. I wanted to fuck. I could gape and squeeze shut. He kneeled, I offered. He touched his lacquered cock's head to my lacquered ass hole. My eyeball. My tail.

"I like this wiggly thing," he said.

"Gimme, gimme," I moaned. "Fuck it!"

I winked from my face and my ass exactly the same. Morris grunted and pushed in, trying to bypass my devil.

"I like that, *mama*. Holy."

I was dirty on the floor there. He kept nudging and trying to push past my tail.

"Keep on wiggling for me, *mama*. I like what you got."

I couldn't see myself. I trusted him to see. Finally his cock pierced my tail with its sticky red and black power. I screamed. Inner ass. Truth doggy-style. My third eye shot open. I sucked his cock with forced clutch. I ground my knees into the burnt earth. Oil slickened my ass. His cock was copper meat. It was mine.

"Morris," I groaned.

He was buried inside me. I could've stayed there forever. His cock in my back. It completed my rise.

"Morris!" I screamed.

He did not know my name.

Morris's hands gripped my waist. His cock fucked through my slick, ticklish cheeks in and out of my ass. Oily piston mama fuck, this was sluicing full of life. *Yoni* love is anal love. If you plug it, man, pulse it, it'll wind like a sweet vine around your hot balls. I licked the salt earth. I exuded grape oils. My thighs were two tree trunks grounded in fire.

Morris held me in position. Sister-sister. I throat-puffed. Every nerve in my system was sparking alive. The power of cunt ridge. Niagara abyss. Ass tail. I spread wide. This was bucking love, manlove! I tried to suction out his semen. My tail found his prostate, I grabbed underneath at his sac. I jiggled and I jiggled. I jiggled his balls and he spurted hot deep up my ass. I moaned and I kept him there squeezing and squeezing. I felt energy rise. Energy fill up my ass. My ass filled the cave. My brain returned.

Morris slid out of my back and immediately lay down to put his face under my pussy. My pussy spasmed lava onto the dent of his head. Flames flickered from the hearth. I started to feel this post-ass-fuck ecstatic instruction. My body was a channel and *it could be spoken to*. I don't know if it was the spiritual wife or Tamara, but a female voice said: *kunt wheel, yoni up.*

I shed my old self completely. I threw

Dana into the fire. And Yoo-hoo, the yogic pleasure machine, sprang up to standing, pussy hot and ass alight. Yoo-hoo did something she never knew she could do. Like a magician, a gymnast, she flipped backwards by herself. Right into a back bend, head towards the fire.

Morris watched me drop. I landed on my hands. My chest cracked, my knees bent. My heart pump-pump-pumped. Kunt wheel, *yoni* up! Kunt wheel, *yoni* up!

"Awesome, *mama*," Morris said.

My nipples burned in *Urdhva Danurasana*. Morris crouched in front of my pussy. Have you ever seen a cunt ready to be tongued in a back bend? Morris's tongue pierce flicked hard back and forth on my clit. Everything prickled, squeezed, and cramped. My heart expanded. And I touched the skull of Morris with my smashed, dripping *kunt*.

"Come on, *mama*, come on, now. . ."

Morris worked his great tongue, whorling throughout my smashed pussy, sucking up all my electricity. He nudged a thick knuckle up my back pussy and lodged a pinky in my sore asshole all at once. He kept flicking my clit with his steel circle tongue. The pinging sound cut through the drone of the falls. Morris pulled on my tail. He did not let me unfold. A wheel spins, a wheel drives. . .

"Come on, *mama*, let it out at me."

"Yass, Morris!"

My cervix spasmed. Bags jiggle. Falls gush. A pussy gushes!

All of my juice, all this life force. . . I

cracked, ejaculating.

Morris shook his bald head. I anointed his dome. I sprayed to the hearth. I prayed to the Earth. For Tamara, for all girls, I prayed: *love thyself, kunt.*

I cuddled with Morris on his tatami mat before the fire.

"I think you know what you're doing," he said.

Exhausted, we slept. I dreamt of a firebombed KIA, and a cock like a stake.

Suddenly, it was sweltering. The sun spread diagonally into the mouth of the cave. I saw two slithering bodies. Bruised little knees. I was sweating profusely. I sat up and stared. The first girl and the second girl in their leopard print bikinis were in the cave, drenched, squatting down in front of me.

"Yoo-hoo," they whispered, "come."

The first girl and the second girl knew my name. I was so happy to see them.

"Tamara sent us," they said. Neither of them smiled.

I realized that they had very strong accents, maybe Eastern European, I didn't know from where. Tamara was up there, waiting for me. Tamara was not ruled by Siddiqui anymore. Tamara had cut the cord. She was free.

"Come on, she's waiting for us," the first girl whispered.

"On the American side," said the second girl.

"We're going to show the world who we are."

"You'll show us how."

I felt wide awake, thrilled. I took each

girl's slithery hand and led them to the corner of the cave where there was a rumpled heap of clothes. Morris grunted in his sleep. The girls giggled.

"We've got to get rid of these bikinis first," I said.

The girls stripped out of their suits. They were like slick little fishes. There was something crackling in their bodies, all the jerking and curving as they released themselves from the bikini uniforms. Their nipples were hard, their pussies hairy and thick. I'd drink pussy juice one day; a diet of pussy juice for clarity. Morris snored. I found army shorts for the girls that came down to their ankles. I tied a rope belt around each of their waists. I slipped army T-shirts over their heads. I gave them each a camouflage hat. I got dressed in one of Morris's green army T-shirts, camouflage flak jacket, and army pants. I took matches from his supplies, plus a hook full of dried fish and a pocket knife. I smelled pussy everywhere. I couldn't wait to see Tamara.

Then me and the girls, hand-in-hand, walked out of the cave. We took the path up towards America.

ABOUT THE AUTHOR

Tamara Faith Berger has published three novels: *Lie With Me* (2001), *The Way of the Whore* (2004), and *Maidenhead* (2012). Her first two novels were recently re-published as *Little Cat* (2013). She has been published in Taddle Creek, Adult, and Apology magazines. Her work has been translated into Spanish and German. Tamara won the Believer Book Award for *Maidenhead*. She lives in Toronto.

Kuntalini
is available as an enhanced ebook
with additional multimedia content for
Apple iBooks and Amazon Kindle

For more information, visit
www.badlandsunlimited.com